Listen, Read, & Learn

Volume 3

The Three Billy Goats Gruff

Cinderella

Peter Pan

The Ugly Duckling

Thinking Kids®
Carson-Dellosa Publishing LLC
Greensboro, North Carolina

Thinking Kids®
Carson-Dellosa Publishing LLC
P.O. Box 35665
Greensboro, NC 27425 USA

ISBN 978-1-4838-3516-7

Table of Contents

 Download Free Audio Files for Read-Aloud Stories in This Volume

To find a free MP3 audio file of each story in this volume, go to carsondellosa.com and search for the product page that matches this book. Search by the title (*Listen, Read, & Learn Volume 3*) or product item number (704734). To download, click the link found under Resources/Downloads.

Listen, Read, & Learn
Introduction

The Value of Classic Stories

Classic fairy tales and folktales from around the world are similar in their themes of good vs. evil and cleverness vs. force or might. The details of the stories may change, but the themes remain universal. Many educators believe that fairy tales are good for children because they represent what all people fear and desire, and thus help children face their own fears and wishes. Children may benefit from hearing stories with some element of danger, and then being reassured with happy endings in which the small, apparently powerless hero or heroine triumphs after all. This is especially true when a supportive parent takes the time to discuss the stories and provide specific, personal reassurance to the child.

Knowing these favorite tales and their famous characters will help your child begin to form a rich knowledge of cultural literacy. Classic stories present diverse cultures, new ideas, and clever problem-solving. They use language in creative and colorful ways and serve as a springboard for your child's imagination. Most of all, classic stories delight and entertain young readers and form a solid base for a lifelong love of literature and reading.

Reading Aloud with Your Child

Young children love to hear favorite stories over and over again, and the classic tales in this volume should be no exception. Have fun with your child telling and retelling these beloved stories in different ways: by reading aloud from the text, by telling the stories from memory, by pausing to let your child insert well-known lines, by making up and performing voices for the characters, and by listening to the audio component (see below).

Whatever approach you choose, make sure to engage your child in the story. You can do this by talking about the story before, during, and after reading. Ask your child to make predictions about what will happen next, to think about what characters are thinking and feeling at different points in the story, and to imagine what might happen to the characters after the story concludes. You can also help your child develop early reading skills by pointing to letters and words on the page. Ask your child to examine words that rhyme, to find a specific letter within a word, or to identify an important word (such as a character's name) and try to locate it on every page.

Using the *Listen, Read, & Learn* Audio Component

Download these convenient MP3 files to your computer, tablet, phone, or other device using the directions provided on page 3 of this book. Then, listen to the lively recordings of the stories in this volume anywhere, at any time—at home or on the go. Encourage your child to chime in with the storyteller during favorite lines from the story. Or, pause the audio and ask your child to tell what happens next in the story.

Activities to Support Early Learning

After telling and retelling each classic tale, invite your child to complete the learning activity pages that follow each story in this book. These age-appropriate activities support your child's understanding of the story. They develop early reading and thinking skills by focusing on these concepts: **Understanding Characters and Events, Predicting Outcomes, Making Personal Connections, Reality vs. Fantasy, Sequencing, Classifying, Comparing and Contrasting, Following Directions, Counting, Letters and Sounds, Rhyming Words**, and **Vocabulary**. As your child completes the activities, encourage him or her to talk about how each one relates to the story.

Cinderella

Retold by Lindsay Mizer   Illustrated by Jim Talbot

Once upon a time, there lived a beautiful young girl named Ella. She was very kind-hearted, even to her stepmother and stepsisters, who treated her terribly. Every day, they made Ella do chores from morning until night while they sat around and did nothing.

Ella didn't mind the hard work. She daydreamed to pass the time. She imagined she was a royal princess dressed in a fine gown, not in her own dress, which was covered with cinders from the fire.

"*Cinder*ella! *Cinder*ella!" her stepsisters would tease her.

But Cinderella was too lost in her dreams to hear them.

One day, a royal messenger dropped off an invitation. All of the ladies in the kingdom were invited to attend a royal ball in honor of the prince.

"Do you know what this means?" shrieked the greedy stepmother. "The prince must be looking for a princess. If he chooses one of you, we all could be royalty."

"Cinderella! Go help your sisters get ready!"

Cinderella carefully sewed her stepsisters' dresses. She gently fixed their hair. And all without so much as a "thank you" from them.

"May I go to the ball with you, too?" Cinderella asked her stepmother quietly.

"Ha!" laughed her stepmother. "What would you wear, Cinderella, that dirty old dress?"

Cinderella begged her stepsisters to lend her a dress for the ball.

"You?" the older stepsister asked. "Borrow my dress? Never!"

"Do you think they want a dirty cinder girl at the ball?" howled the younger stepsister.

"Besides," said her stepmother, "you have a lot of work to do here. Clean the curtains and mop the floors while we're gone."

After her family left, Cinderella burst into tears. How she wished she could go to the ball!

"Don't cry, sweet girl," squeaked a tiny voice. Cinderella turned to find a small, sparkly fairy looking at her. "I am your fairy godmother. And if you wish to go to the ball, then you shall go. Now, let's get to work!"

"First, fetch me a pumpkin, Cinderella, and clean it out," said the fairy godmother.

"Now, fetch me some mice."

Swoosh! With the wave of her wand, Cinderella's fairy godmother turned the pumpkin into a beautiful coach and the mice into elegant footmen.

"Oh!" cried Cinderella. "It's beautiful. But look at me. I have nothing to wear but these dirty rags."

"Well," said her fairy godmother, "I can fix that."

Suddenly, Cinderella's ragged dress turned into a long, flowing gown. On her feet were a pair of sparkling glass slippers.

"Thank you, Fairy Godmother," said Cinderella.

"Enjoy the ball, my child," said her fairy godmother. "But remember this. At the stroke of midnight, all of the magic will disappear."

Cinderella arrived at the palace in high style. She caught the eye of the handsome prince, and they spent the entire night dancing, talking, and gazing into one another's eyes.

"Who is this mysterious girl?" whispered the guests. "Where did she come from?"

Bong! The clock startled Cinderella. It was almost midnight! She gave the prince one last loving look and ran out of the ballroom.

"Wait!" cried the prince. "I must know your name. I want to…." But Cinderella had already disappeared, leaving behind only a glass slipper on the palace steps.

"Poor Cinderella!" taunted her stepsister the next morning.

"You missed it. The prince danced all night with a beautiful princess. She and I became good friends!"

Cinderella smiled knowingly.

"I hear the prince is conducting a search for the mysterious princess. Whoever fits the glass slipper she left behind will become his wife."

That afternoon, a royal messenger arrived at Cinderella's house. The stepsisters tried to squeeze their feet into the glass slipper, but their feet were much too big.

"May I try on the glass slipper?" asked
Cinderella.

"No!" screamed the angry stepsisters. "Go away."

"Wait a minute," said the royal messenger. "Every woman in the kingdom must try on the slipper, Prince's orders."

Cinderella carefully slid her foot into the glass slipper. It fit perfectly! Suddenly, her ragged dress turned into a beautiful ball gown.

"Thank you, Fairy Godmother," whispered Cinderella, "wherever you are."

Cinderella married the prince on a beautiful sunny day. She never returned to her stepmother's house or scrubbed another floor after that. And she and the prince lived happily ever after together in his palace.

The End

The Puppets Tell the Story

Cut out the puppets on this page and on page 41. Glue each one to the top of a craft stick. Use the puppets to retell "Cinderella."

Cinderella

Cinderella

Make a Book

Cut out the mini-pages. Put them in order to make a book that tells the story of "Cinderella." Staple your book together. Read it to a friend.

Cinderella

She did chores all day long.

When Cinderella cried, her fairy godmother appeared.

Racing to get home by midnight, Cinderella dropped her shoe.

Make a Book (Part 2)

All the ladies were invited to the ball. Cinderella had nothing to wear.

Cinderella's stepmother and stepsisters were mean to her.

The prince promised to marry the lady who fit the glass slipper. He and Cinderella lived happily ever after.

Thanks to the fairy godmother's magic, Cinderella went to the ball and danced with the prince.

Chore Choices

Help Cinderella finish her work so she can go to the ball. Circle each picture that shows something Cinderella will need to do chores around the house.

Presto!

Imagine that a fairy godmother used magic to change a pumpkin into something else just for you. What would it be? Draw a picture to show your idea. Then, write a sentence to tell about your picture.

What to Wear?

Imagine you are invited to the royal ball. What will you wear? Draw a picture of yourself all dressed up for the ball. Then, write a sentence to tell about your picture.

Cinderella

They Are the Same

Look at the first picture in each row. Circle the picture that is the **same**.

They Are Different

Look at the first picture in each row. Circle the picture that is **different**.

It Is Magic

The fairy godmother used magic to help Cinderella go to the ball. Draw a line to show how each thing was changed.

Skill: Understanding Characters and Events

Magic Words

Choose letters near the fairy godmother's wand. Write them in the spaces to change the old words into new words!

Cinderella

wand _____

wan_____

_____ wish

_____ish

rag _____

ra_____

hold

_____old

_____ run

_____un

h n d
g f
t

_____ mouse

_____ouse

Fairy Tale Words

Write a word to name each picture.

| castle | prince | fairy | wand | coach | crown |

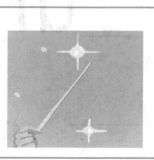

More Than One

Decide if each picture shows one or more than one. Circle the correct word. Then, write it in the blank.

Cinderella

_____

sister   sisters

bow   bows

_____

dress   dresses

stool   stools

_____

mouse   mice

brush   brushes

B Is for Ball

At the ball, Cinderella danced with the prince. The word **ball** begins with **b**. Say the name of each picture. If it begins with the sound of **b**, write **b** on the line.

P Is for Pumpkin

The fairy godmother changed a pumpkin into a coach.
The word **pumpkin** begins with **p**. Say the name of each
picture. If it begins with the sound of **p**, write **p** on the line.

Cinderella

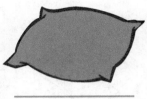

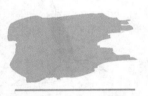

Listen for Short o

You hear the sound of **short o** in the middle of the word **clock**.
Write a **short o** word to describe each picture.

on	off	hot	mop	top	clock

At Midnight

At midnight, the fairy godmother's magic came to an end. When it is late at night and both hands of the clock are on 12, it is twelve o'clock, or midnight. Look at the clock that shows midnight. Write the missing numbers.

Real or Make-Believe?

Some events that happen in fairy tales like "Cinderella" could not happen in real life. Describe what is happening in each picture. Draw an **X** on the pictures that show things that could not really happen.

PETER PAN

RETOLD BY CAROL OTTOLENGHI   ILLUSTRATED BY SHELLEY BRANT

Long ago, the Darling family lived in London. Every night, Mrs. Darling told her three children, Wendy, John, and Michael, exciting stories about an island with pirates and Indians. Sometimes, she felt as if someone else was listening to her stories. One night, she saw him!

Mrs. Darling laid a trap to catch the sneaky listener. She did not catch him, but she did catch his shadow! She showed it to her husband, Mr. Darling.

"Very good, my dear," he said. "It must have been a burglar. Well, he won't be back. You scared him off."

Two nights later, Mr. and Mrs. Darling went to a party.

"Oh, Mother!" said Wendy. "You look beautiful. When may I wear a dress like that?"

"You may wear one when you are all grown up," said Mrs. Darling. "Just don't grow up too fast." Then, she and Mr. Darling kissed their children and left.

Later that night, Wendy heard someone crying. It wasn't her brother John. It wasn't her brother Michael. It was a boy she had never seen before!

"Why are you crying?" Wendy asked the boy.

"My shadow won't stay on anymore!" cried the boy.

"Well, I can sew your shadow to your feet," said Wendy. "But first, tell me who you are."

"I am Peter Pan!" said the boy.

Wendy finished sewing on the shadow, and Peter Pan leapt to his feet. "Thank you!" he said. "I flew here. As a reward for helping me, you and your brothers can fly with me to Neverland."

He sprinkled Wendy, John, and Michael with fairy dust from his friend Tinker Bell. And what do you know? They could fly!

As they flew high above the other houses, Wendy asked, "Why were you at our house, Peter?"

"I like to hear your mother's stories," said Peter. "Do you know any stories?"

"Of course," said Wendy.

"Then, you can be Mother to the Lost Boys and tell us stories. Look," Peter pointed, "Neverland!"

Tinker Bell felt jealous. "Peter is my friend," she said to herself. "Not Wendy's."

Tinker Bell told the Lost Boys that Wendy was a giant bird. "Peter wants you to shoot it down with arrows," she said. So, the Lost Boys knocked Wendy out of the sky.

But Peter was furious! "This girl was going to be our mother and tell us stories," he told them. The Lost Boys felt very bad. They built Wendy a house to stay in while she recovered.

When Wendy was feeling better, they all set off to rescue Tiger Lily, the Indian princess, who had been captured by pirates.

The captain of the pirates was Captain Hook. He hated the Lost Boys, Peter Pan, and crocodiles. Long ago, he had been holding a clock when a crocodile jumped out of the water and bit off his hand. Now, Captain Hook had a hook for a left hand, and the crocodile sounded like *tick-tock, tick-tock*!

While Peter and Hook fought, Wendy and the Lost Boys rescued Tiger Lily. Captain Hook slashed Peter with his hook before Peter could get away.

Life at Neverland was exciting, but John and Michael were homesick. "We miss Mother and Father," they told Wendy.

"We are going home, and the Lost Boys are coming with us," Wendy told Peter. "You may come, too."

"No!" Peter yelled. "I would have to grow up!" Wendy gave Peter some medicine. "This will make your cut better. Make sure you take it."

Wendy and the boys left, but they did not get far! The pirates captured them one by one as they climbed out of the tree house.

"Take them to the ship!" Captain Hook told the other pirates.

Then, Captain Hook snuck into the tree house and poured poison into Peter's medicine!

"This will be wonderful," Captain Hook told Wendy. "The boys shall be pirates, and you shall be our mother."

"Never!" Wendy yelled. "Peter Pan will rescue us."

"No, he won't," said Captain Hook. "I poisoned his medicine. Very soon, Peter Pan will be dead!"

Tinker Bell heard this. "I must warn Peter!" she said to herself.

Tinker Bell sped to the tree house. She broke the medicine bottle and told Peter what was happening. "We must rescue them!" Peter cried.

But Captain Hook was very angry at Wendy and the boys. "If you will not be our mother and tell us stories, then the boys must walk the plank!" he said.

Suddenly, there was a loud *tick-tock, tick-tock*.

"No!" cried Captain Hook. "It is the crocodile. It has come back to eat the rest of me."

"I hope the crocodile is hungry!" cried Peter Pan, as he jumped onto the deck.

Tinker Bell sprinkled the other pirates with fairy dust. They floated into the air and could not help their captain.

Peter Pan and Captain Hook wrestled back and forth. Finally, Peter gave a huge push…and pushed Hook overboard!

Peter and Tinker Bell took Wendy, John, Michael, and all of the Lost Boys to the Darlings' home.

"We are glad you came back," cried Mrs. Darling. "We missed you so much."

"May the Lost Boys stay with us?" Wendy asked.

"Of course," said Mr. Darling.

Peter never came to stay with them. But sometimes he would visit…

...when Mrs. Darling was telling stories.

The Puppets Tell the Story

Cut out the puppets on this page and on page 93. Glue each one to the top of a craft stick. Use the puppets to retell "Peter Pan."

Peter Pan

Peter Pan

If You Could Fly

Imagine that Tinker Bell sprinkled some fairy dust on you so that you could fly. Where would you go? Draw a picture to show your idea. Then, write a sentence about it.

Peter Pan

What Happened First?

Look at the pictures in each row. Circle the one that shows what happened **first** in "Peter Pan."

What Happened Last?

Look at the pictures in each row. Circle the one that shows what happened **last** in "Peter Pan."

What If?

What if the events in "Peter Pan" had happened differently?
Draw a picture to show your answer to each question.

What if Mrs. Darling had not caught Peter Pan listening?

What if Peter had decided to grow up?

What if Captain Hook had not captured the children?

Where Does It Belong?

Look at each picture. If it shows something that belongs in the Darlings' home, circle it. If it shows something that belongs in Neverland, draw a square around it.

Peter Pan

Shadow Match

Draw a line to match each character with a shadow.

Real or Make-Believe?

Look at each picture. If it shows something that could happen in real life, write **R** on the line. If it shows something that is pretend or make-believe, write **M** on the line.

_____

- - - - - - -

_____

_____

- - - - - - -

_____

_____

- - - - - - -

_____

_____

- - - - - - -

_____

_____

- - - - - - -

_____

_____

- - - - - - -

_____

This Is Neverland

Use the space to draw a map of the island of Neverland. Include each place shown in the map key. Use your map to answer the questions on page 103.

Key

= Sea

= Land

= Ship

= Wendy's House

= Tree House

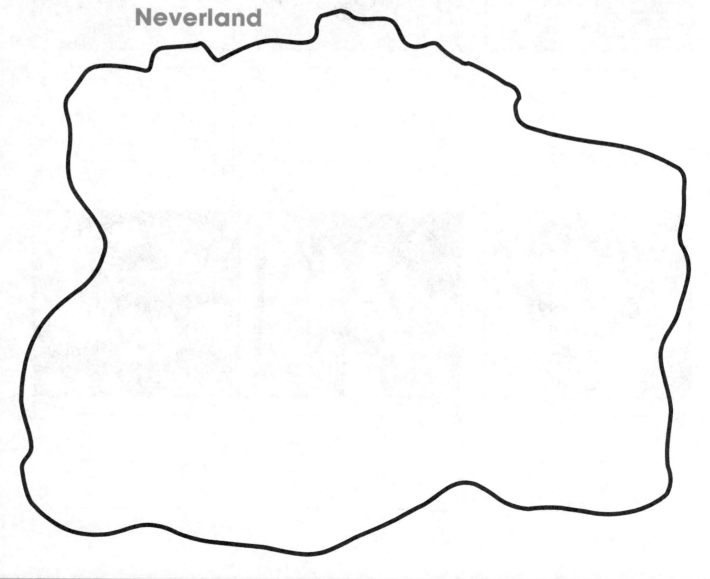

Neverland

This Is Neverland (Part 2)

What is on the sea?

_____

- -

_____

What is beside Wendy's house?

_____

- -

_____

Where does Peter Pan live?

_____

- -

_____

What place is farthest away from the tree house?

_____

- -

_____

What place is closest to Captain Hook's ship?

_____

- -

_____

Peter Pan

W Is for Wendy

The name **Wendy** begins with **w**. Say the name of each picture.
If it begins with the sound of **w**, write **w** on the line.

H Is for Hook

Hook begins with **h**. Say the name of each picture. If it begins with the sound of **h**, write **h** on the line.

Peter Pan

_____

- - - - - - - - -

_____

_____

- - - - - - - - -

_____

_____

- - - - - - - - -

_____

_____

- - - - - - - - -

_____

Listen for Short a

Peter Pan never wants to grow up. You hear the sound of **short a** in the middle of **Pan**. Say the name of each picture. Circle the pictures that have the sound of **short a**.

A Rhyming Game

Cut out the cards and lay them facedown. Turn over any two cards and read the words. Do the words rhyme? If they do, keep them and turn over two more cards.

ship

tree

hook

lip

book

boat

coat

bee

The Three Billy Goats Gruff

Retold by Carol Ottolenghi

Illustrated by Joshua Janes

Once upon a time, there were three billy goats named Gruff. There was Little Billy Goat Gruff. There was Middle Billy Goat Gruff. And there was Big Billy Goat Gruff.

The Billy Goats Gruff lived in a big, grassy meadow. A stream cut through the meadow, and a bridge crossed over the stream. In the stream, under the bridge, lived…

...A TROLL!

He was a snarling, sneaky, big bad bully of a troll. And when anyone wanted to cross the bridge, he would ram them with his club. Then, he would eat them up.

This was a problem for the Billy Goats Gruff. Their side of the meadow had lovely green grass. But there was even greener grass on the other side of the bridge.

So, the three Billy Goats Gruff came up with a plan. Then, they sent the littlest goat across the bridge.

Little Billy Goat Gruff's hooves tip-tapped softly on the bridge.

The troll roared. "How dare you tip-tap across my bridge?" he hollered. "I am going to eat you!"

"Don't be silly," said Little Billy Goat Gruff. "I'm a very little goat, not much of a meal for a big troll like you. There's a much bigger goat coming behind me."

"Humph," said the troll. "Maybe I'll wait for the bigger goat."

The troll hid under the bridge to wait, and Little Billy Goat Gruff ran into the meadow.

"Our plan is working," Middle Billy Goat Gruff said to Big Billy Goat Gruff. "It's my turn."

He started to cross the bridge. His hooves clip-clopped sharply on the wood.

123

The troll roared and waved his club. "How dare you clip-clop across my bridge?" he hollered. "I am..."

"Quit being a bully!" Middle Billy Goat Gruff told him. "This is not your bridge. And I am not much of a meal for a troll like you. There is a much larger goat coming soon."

"I am not a bully!" said the troll.

"Are you stronger than me?" demanded Middle Billy Goat Gruff. "And are you picking on me?"

"Humph," grumbled the troll. "I'm going to wait for the bigger goat."

127

Now, it's my turn, Big Billy Goat Gruff thought to himself.

His wide feet pounded across the bridge.

"I wonder what that bully of a troll will do now," Big Billy Goat Gruff said to himself. He stomped his feet a little louder. "Maybe he will leave me alone."

But there was a roar from under the bridge.
"Who's that stomping across my bridge?"
bellowed the troll. He was now very cranky and
very hungry.

"I am Big Billy Goat Gruff," said the goat. "And I want to cross this bridge."

"I am Troll," said the grumpy old troll. "And I want to eat you up!"

Big Billy Goat Gruff snorted and waved his horns as he charged the troll. The troll growled and howled as he charged the big goat. They slammed into each other with an awful crash!

139

And the troll who lived under the bridge never bullied anyone again.

The Puppets Tell the Story

Cut out the puppets on this page and on page 143. Glue each one to the top of a craft stick. Use the puppets to retell "The Three Billy Goats Gruff."

The
Three
Billy Goats
Gruff

Think Back

Say the name of each picture. Then, think back to the story "The Three Billy Goats Gruff." Circle the pictures of things that were in the story.

The Order of the Story

Write **1** next to the picture that shows what happened first in "The Three Billy Goats Gruff." Write **2** and **3** next to the pictures that show what happened next. Write **4** next to the picture that shows what happened last in the story.

A Visit from the Billy Goats

Pretend that the three billy goats came clip-clopping up to your door asking for something good to eat. What might happen next? Draw a picture to show your idea. Then, write a sentence about it.

The
Three
Billy Goats
Gruff

Big and Little

One billy goat was big and one was little. **Big** and **little** are opposites. Draw lines to connect the pictures that show opposites.

Small, Medium, or Large?

Cut out the pictures and sort them by size. Then, tape or glue each one in the correct place to complete the chart on page 151.

The Three Billy Goats Gruff

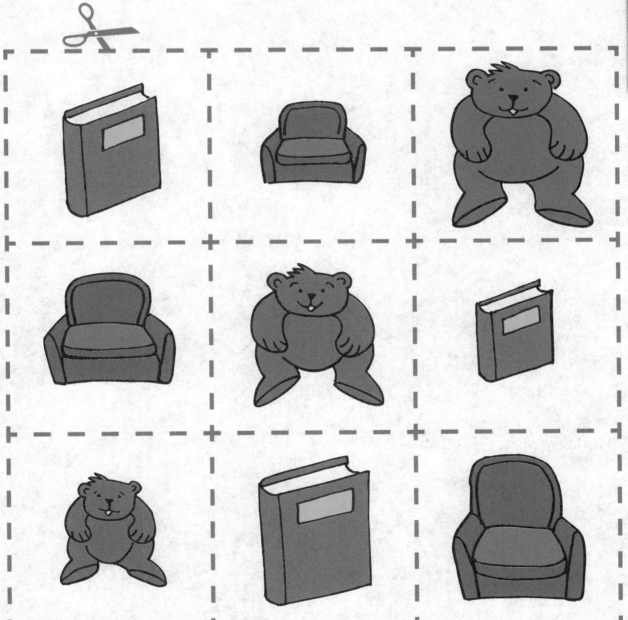

Small, Medium, or Large? (Part 2)

Small	Medium	Large

The Three Billy Goats Gruff

What's Next?

After billy goats eat grass, they play! Look at the goat in each box. Circle the picture that shows what the goat will do next.

What's Different?

Look closely at the two pictures. They are not the same! Circle four things in the bottom picture that are different from the top picture.

The Three Billy Goats Gruff

G Is for Goat

The word **goat** begins with the sound of **g**. Say the name of each picture. If it begins with the sound of **g**, write **g** on the line.

R Is for Roar

The troll roared at the goats. The word **roar** begins with the sound of **r**. Write **r** to complete each word that has the sound of **r**.

st___eam

 ___ock

t___oll

flowe___

b___idge

t___ee

Listen for Short u

You hear the **short u** sound in the middle of the name **Gruff**.
Say the name of each picture. If you hear the **short u** sound in
the middle of the word, write **u** on the line.

Find a Rhyme

Say the names of the pictures in each row. Color the pictures whose names rhyme.

The Three Billy Goats Gruff

  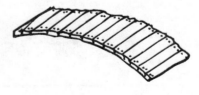

Words I Can Read

Read the words on the bridge. They are often used in stories.
Trace the words to complete the sentences.

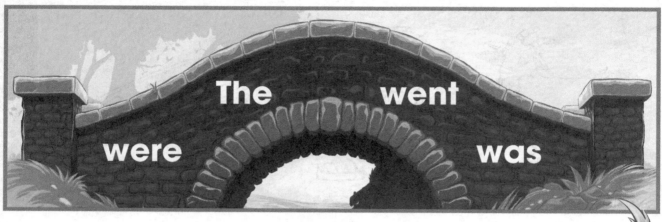

There _____ were _____ three goats.

The _____ goats ate grass.

They _____ went _____ to the stream.

There _____ was _____ a troll.

The Ugly Duckling

Retold by Claire Daniel

Illustrated by Tammy Ortner

One fine spring day, a mother duck sat on some eggs in her nest. She wanted to keep the eggs warm. She sat quietly and waited for them to hatch.

The mother duck had five eggs in her nest. Four of the eggs were small. The fifth egg was very big.

Then one day, the eggs began to crack. One, two, three, four small eggs hatched. But the biggest egg did not hatch.

So the mother duck sat down again. She kept the biggest egg warm. She waited for it to hatch, too.

Finally, the big egg began to crack. The last duckling popped out.

"Cheep! Cheep!" he said.

The mother duck stared at the baby bird's long neck. She looked at his gray feathers. She looked at the other ducklings.

"He is not like the others," she thought. "But, he is my little duckling, and I love him very much."

During the summer, the mother duck wanted to teach her ducklings to swim. She walked to the water. The four yellow ducklings followed her. So did the little gray duckling.

"What is that ugly thing?" said the other ducks at the pond.

"Leave him alone!" the mother duck said. "He is my little duckling. He can swim. He is big and strong. He'll be a handsome duck one day."

But the ducks did not leave him alone. They hissed and pecked at him. They called him "the ugly duckling." So he decided to run away.

The ugly duckling swam up the river. There, he met some wild ducks.

But there were hunters nearby. They fired shots at the ducks. The ugly duckling was very frightened.

The wild ducks flew up and away. And the ugly
duckling was alone again.

The ugly duckling swam on up the river.
Soon, he came to a cottage. He was very tired.
He lay down and went to sleep.

The next morning, an old woman found the ugly duckling.

"I'm so glad you are here!" she said. "You can be a big help. Come meet the other animals."

The ugly duckling was very happy. He had found a place where he was wanted!

"Can you lay eggs?" the hen asked.
"No," said the ugly duckling.
"Can you catch mice?" asked the cat.
"No," said the duckling.
"Then, what good are you?" asked the hen.

The ugly duckling had no answer.
He felt very sad. So he went back
to the river.

The ugly duckling swam and swam. He caught fish to eat. He grew bigger and stronger. But, he was very lonely.

One day in the chilly fall, the ugly duckling saw some beautiful birds in the sky. They were snowy white. They had long, slender necks. How he wished he could fly with them!

Winter came, and the ugly duckling found a small pond where he could stay. But, it got colder and colder. It snowed and snowed.

Then one day, the ugly duckling found that he could not swim. The pond had frozen. He was stuck in the ice!

A woodcutter saw the ugly duckling
stuck in the ice. The woodcutter
chopped away the ice. He took the
duckling home.

The woodcutter put the duckling in front of the fire. Soon, the ugly duckling was warm and happy.

The next day, the ugly duckling felt better. But the woodcutter's children wanted to play. They chased the duckling all around the house until he flew out the door.

Many more days passed. The ugly duckling became cold and hungry.

Then one day, a warm breeze blew. Spring was coming! The ugly duckling looked up at the sky. He wanted to fly. So he raised his wings, and up he went.

As he flew, the ugly duckling saw some beautiful white birds down below. They were swimming in a pond.

The ugly duckling said, "How beautiful they are! I want to swim with them."

The ugly duckling flew down to the water. The beautiful white birds all came swimming toward him. The ugly duckling was frightened.

"Please don't hurt me," said the ugly duckling. "I know I am very ugly."

One of the birds said, "How could you be ugly? You are a swan! And swans are beautiful!"

The ugly duckling looked at himself in the water. He saw not an ugly duckling, but a beautiful swan!

"Look!" cried a little girl from the shore. "Look at the new swan! He's the most beautiful one of all!"

The new swan raised his wings. All the children came to look at him.

The ugly duckling had been very unhappy. But, now he knew that he belonged with the beautiful swans. At last, he was very happy.

The Puppets Tell the Story

Cut out the puppets on this page and on page 193. Glue each one to the top of a craft stick. Use the puppets to retell "The Ugly Duckling."

The
Ugly
Duckling

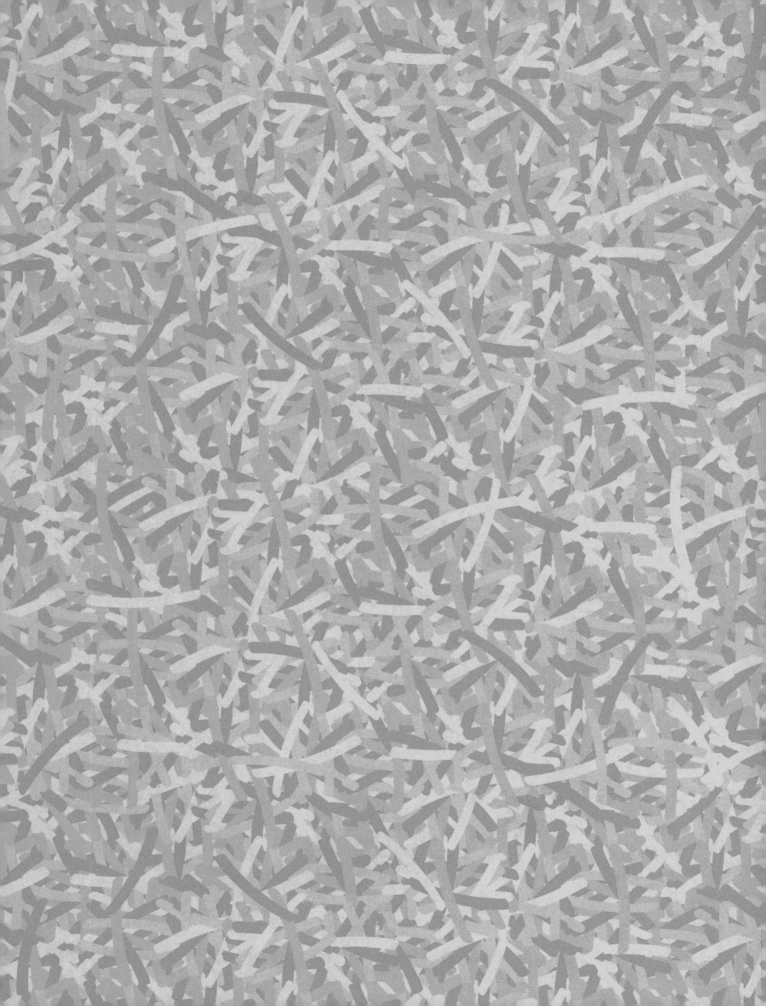

The Ugly Duckling

Story Cards

Cut out the cards on this page and on page 197. Arrange them in the correct order to tell the story "The Ugly Duckling." Glue or tape them in order onto another sheet of paper. Then, use the pictures to tell the story to a friend.

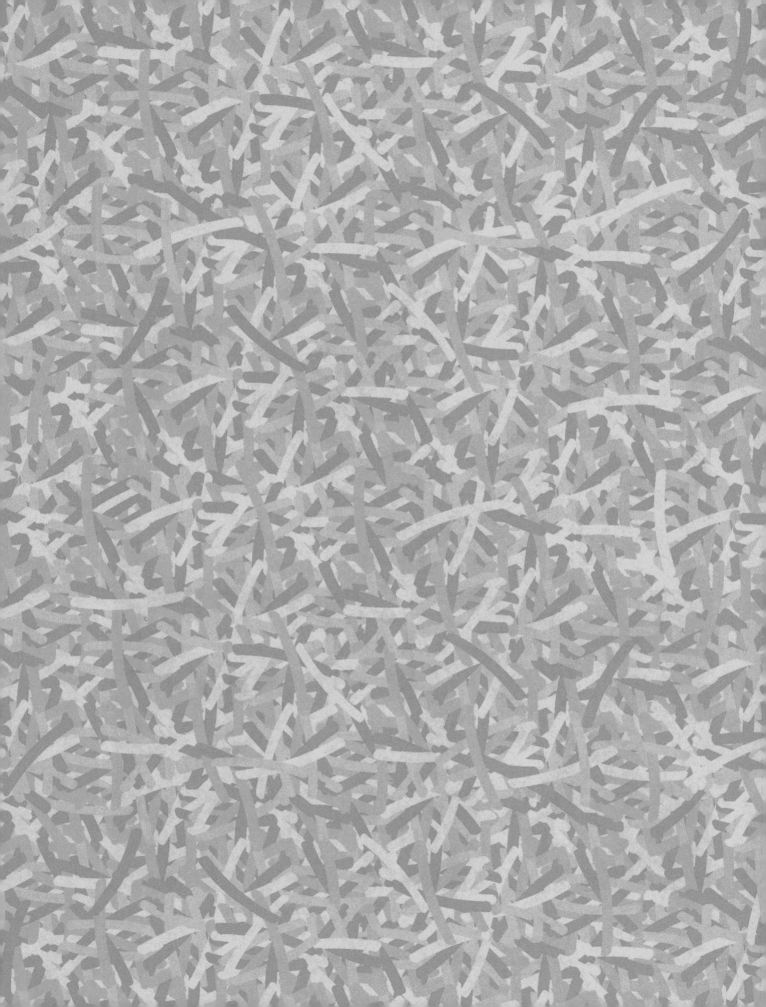

The Ugly Duckling

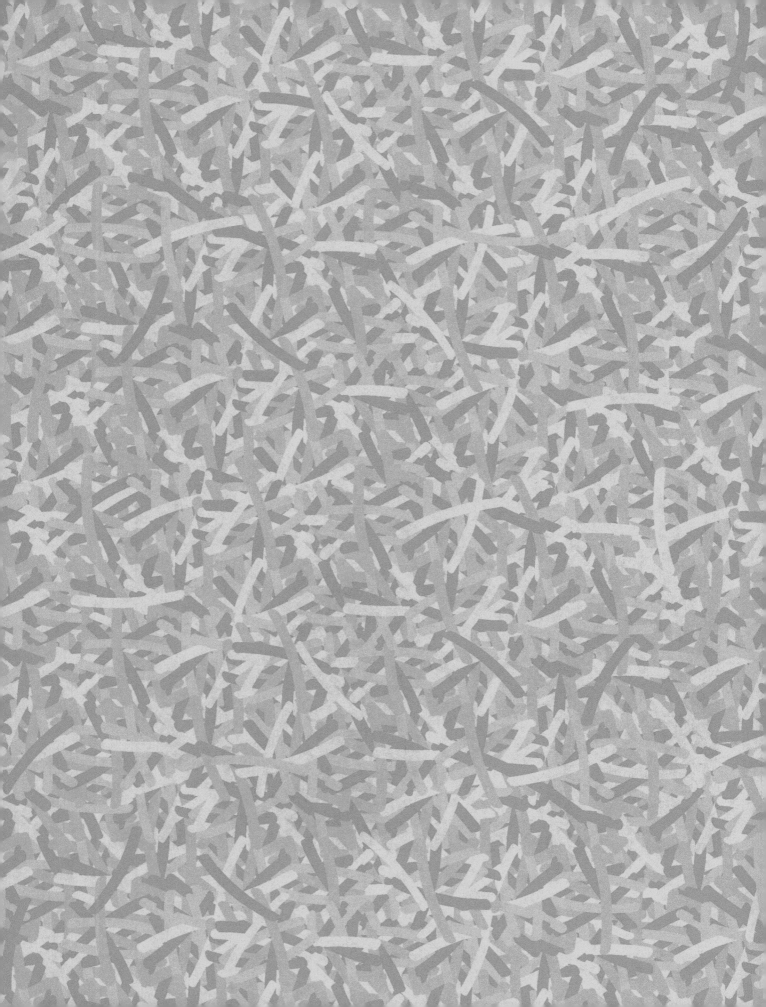

Nice or Not?

Look at each character from "The Ugly Duckling." If the character was nice and helpful to the ugly duckling, draw a happy face in the circle. If the character was unkind to the ugly duckling, draw a sad face in the circle.

The Ugly Duckling and You

Imagine that you found the ugly duckling near your home, alone and afraid. What would you do to help the ugly duckling? Draw your idea. Use the lines to write a sentence about your drawing.

Where Does It Belong?

Look at the first picture in each row. Circle the picture that shows where it belongs.

The Ugly Duckling

Four Seasons

Remember the story "The Ugly Duckling." What events from the story happened in the winter? What happened in the spring? Look at the pictures. Write a word from the box to tell when each event happened.

winter	spring	summer	fall

_____

- - - - - - - - - - - - - - - - -

_____

_____

- - - - - - - - - - - - - - - - -

_____

What Color?

Draw a line from each color name to a picture that should be that color. Then, color the pictures.

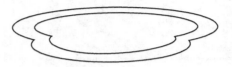

yellow

green

white

blue

How Many Eggs?

Count the eggs in the nest. Write a number on each egg.

| 1 | 2 | 3 | 4 | 5 |

Surprise!

Look at each egg. Draw a picture of the animal you think might hatch from the egg.

The Ugly Duckling

D Is for Duck

You hear the sound of **d** at the beginning of **duck**. Write **d** to complete each word with the **d** sound.

_____

_ _ _ _ _

_____ uckling

_____

_ _ _ _ _

pon _____

_____

_ _ _ _ _

_____ aisy

_____

sa _____

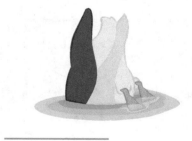

_____

_ _ _ _ _

_____ ive

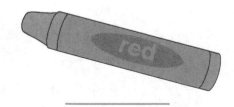

_____

_ _ _ _ _

re _____

F Is for Feather

You hear the sound of **f** at the beginning of **feather**. Say the name of each picture. Circle the pictures that begin with the sound of **f**.

Listen for Short e

You hear the **short e** sound in the middle of **nest**. Say the name of the picture on each egg. If you hear the **short e** sound, color the egg to help it hatch!

Listen for Short i

You hear the **short i** sound in the middle of **swim**. Write **i** to finish each word with the sound of **short i**.

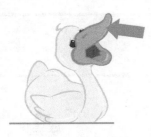

b _ _ _ _ ll

spr _ _ _ _ n g

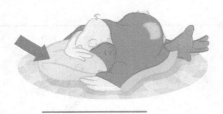

p _ _ _ _ llow

w _ _ _ _ n g

w _ _ _ _ nter

_ _ _ _ n

Animal Names

Write a word from the box to name each animal from "The Ugly Duckling."

swan	duckling	frog	cat	duck	hen

Answer Key

Page 43

Page 44

Page 45

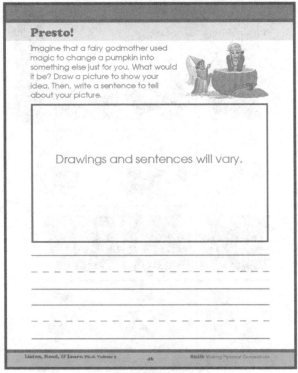

Page 46

Answer Key

Page 47

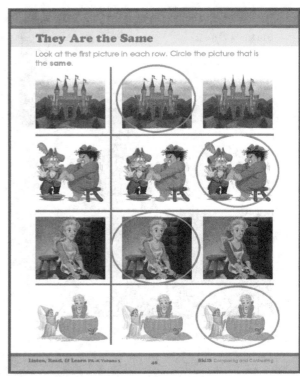

Page 48

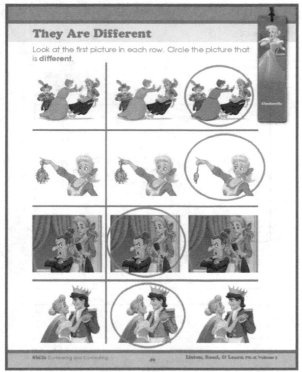

Page 49

Page 50

Answer Key

Magic Words

Choose letters near the fairy godmother's wand. Write them in the spaces to change the old words into new words! Possible answers shown.

wand — wan **t**

wish — **d** ish

rag — ra **n**

hold — **g** old

run — **f** un

mouse — **h** ouse

Page 51

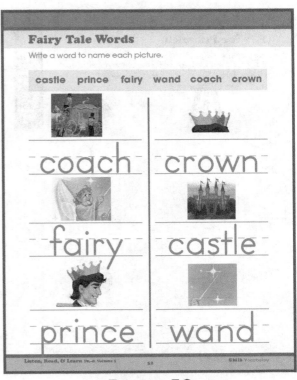

Fairy Tale Words

Write a word to name each picture.

castle   prince   fairy   wand   coach   crown

coach   crown

fairy   castle

prince   wand

Page 52

More Than One

Decide if each picture shows one or more than one. Circle the correct word. Then, write it in the blank.

sisters
sister — (sisters)

bow
(bow) — bows

dresses
dress — (dresses)

stool
(stool) — stools

mice
mouse — (mice)

brush
(brush) — brushes

Page 53

B Is for Ball

At the ball, Cinderella danced with the prince. The word **ball** begins with **b**. Say the name of each picture. If it begins with the sound of **b**, write **b** on the line.

b

b

b

Page 54

Answer Key

Page 55

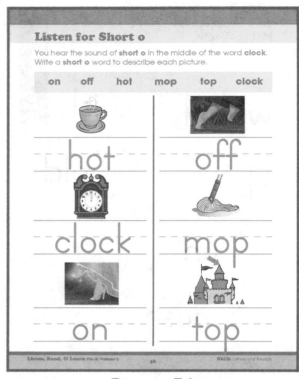

Page 56

Page 57

Page 58

Answer Key

Page 95

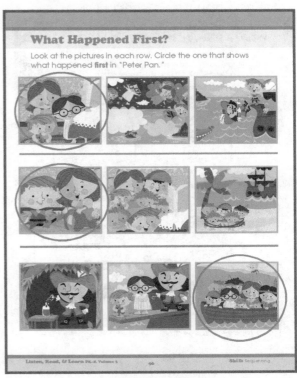

Page 96

Page 97

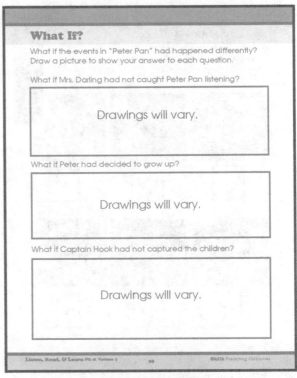

Page 98

Answer Key

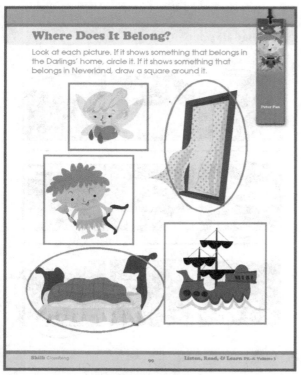

Page 99

Page 100

Page 101

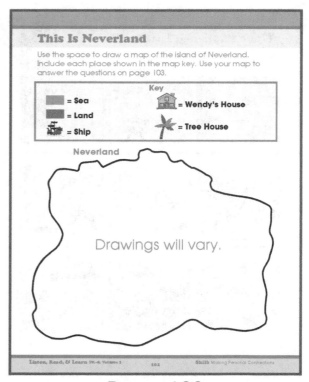

Page 102

Answer Key

This Is Neverland (Part 2)

What is on the sea?

Answers will vary.

What is beside Wendy's house?

Where does Peter Pan live?

What place is farthest away from the tree house?

What place is closest to Captain Hook's ship?

Page 103

W Is for Wendy

The name **Wendy** begins with **w**. Say the name of each picture. If it begins with the sound of **w**, write **w** on the line.

Page 104

H Is for Hook

Hook begins with **h**. Say the name of each picture. If it begins with the sound of **h**, write **h** on the line.

Page 105

Listen for Short a

Peter Pan never wants to grow up. You hear the sound of **short a** in the middle of **Pan**. Say the name of each picture. Circle the pictures that have the sound of **short a**.

Page 106

Answer Key

A Rhyming Game

Cut out the cards and lay them facedown. Turn over any two cards and read the words. Do the words rhyme? If they do, keep them and turn over two more cards.

Page 107

Think Back

Say the name of each picture. Then, think back to the story "The Three Billy Goats Gruff." Circle the pictures of things that were in the story.

Page 145

The Order of the Story

Write **1** next to the picture that shows what happened first in "The Three Billy Goats Gruff." Write **2** and **3** next to the pictures that show what happened next. Write **4** next to the picture that shows what happened last in the story.

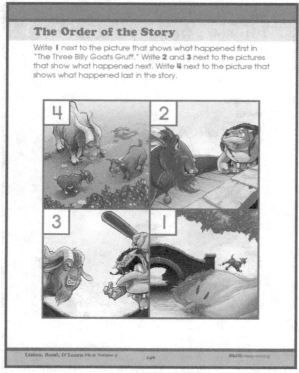

Page 146

A Visit from the Billy Goats

Pretend that the three billy goats came clip-clopping up to your door asking for something good to eat. What might happen next? Draw a picture to show your idea. Then, write a sentence about it.

Drawings and sentences will vary.

Page 147

Answer Key

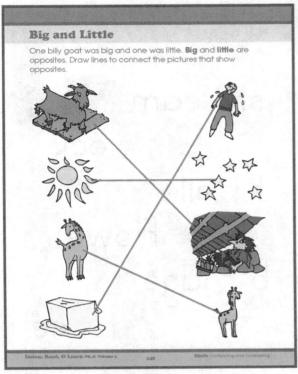

Page 148

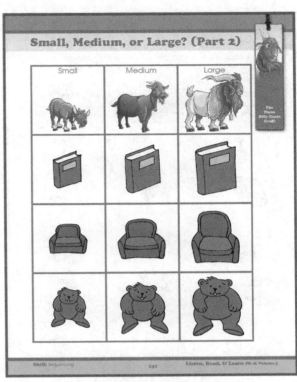

Page 151

Page 152

Page 153

Answer Key

Page 154

Page 155

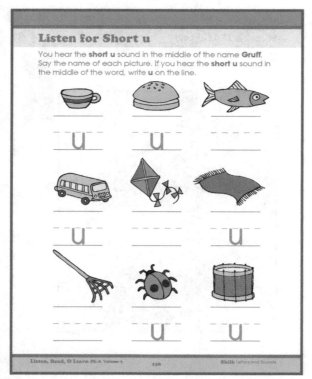

Page 156

Page 157

Answer Key

Page 158

Page 195

Page 197

Page 199

Answer Key

The Ugly Duckling and You

Imagine that you found the ugly duckling near your home, alone and afraid. What would you do to help the ugly duckling? Draw your idea. Use the lines to write a sentence about your drawing.

Drawings and sentences will vary.

Page 200

Where Does It Belong?

Look at the first picture in each row. Circle the picture that shows where it belongs.

Page 201

Four Seasons

Remember the story "The Ugly Duckling." What events from the story happened in the winter? What happened in the spring? Look at the pictures. Write a word from the box to tell when each event happened.

winter   spring   summer   fall

Page 202

What Color?

Draw a line from each color name to a picture that should be that color. Then, color the pictures.

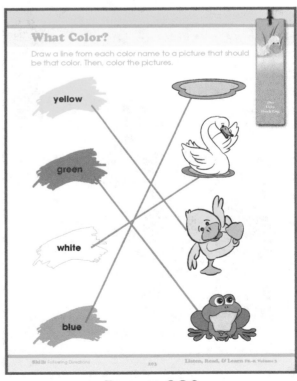

yellow
green
white
blue

Page 203

Answer Key

Page 204

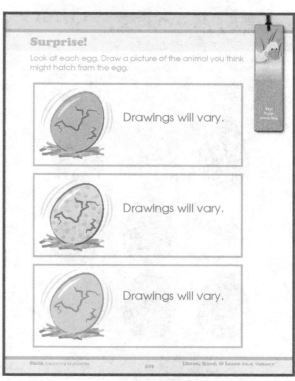

Page 205

Page 206

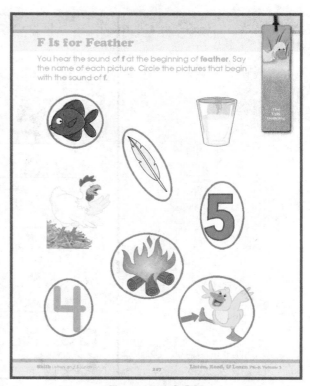

Page 207

Answer Key

Page 208

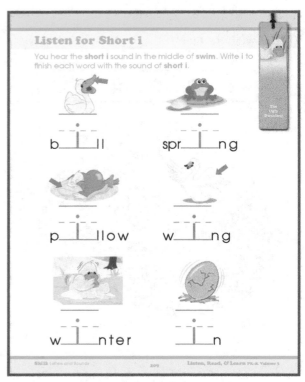

Page 209

Page 210